This book belongs to:

. . . .

. . . .

Quarto is the authority on a wide range of topics.

Quarto educates, entertains and enriches the lives of our readers—enthusiasts and lovers of hands-on living.

www.quartoknows.com

Publisher: Maxime Boucknooghe
Editorial Director: Victoria Garrard
Art Director: Miranda Snow
Series Designer: Victoria Kimonidou
Designer: Chris Fraser
Editor: Joanna McInerney

First published in the UK in 2016
by QED Publishing
Part of The Quarto Group
The Old Brewery
6 Blundell Street
London N7 9BH

A catalogue record for this book is available from the British Library.

ISBN 978 1 78493 533 7

Printed in China

You're Not Ugly, Duckling!

Written by **Steve Smallman**

Illustrated by **Neil Price**

O nce upon a time Mummy Duck sat waiting for her eggs to hatch.

At last,

crack,

crack,

CRACK!

Out popped four adorable ducklings.

But one of the eggs
didn't hatch. Mummy Duck
waited and waited
and waited, until...

...CRACK!

Out came a duckling who was,
well, a little bit different.

He wasn't cute or fluffy and
he had a rather silly hairdo!

Mummy Duck was a bit
surprised but she loved
her baby just the same.

"I think I'll call you Tufty,"
she said, with a smile.

All the cute little ducklings waddled in a line behind their mum but Tufty plodded along on his big flappy feet.

PEEP! PEEP!

"Peep, peep!"
went the little ducklings.

PEEP! PEEP!

"QUAAAARK!"
went Tufty.

"Ugh! What an ugly duckling!"
cried the other animals in the farmyard.

They laughed at him and chased him around,
pecking at his tail and his tufty hair.

"Leave him alone!" cried Mummy
Duck. "You big bullies!"

But it wasn't just big bullies
that poor Tufty had to deal with.
His brothers and sisters bullied him, too.

"Stop that!" shouted a little sparrow. But they took no notice of her.

Tufty got sadder and sadder until, one day...

...he ran away. He left a note for Sparrow.

"Look at this!" cried Sparrow to the
ducklings. "See what you've done!"

The ducklings
felt terrible.

I've gone to find
somewhere I can
really fit in.

Tufty x

They looked everywhere for Tufty but they couldn't find him.

It was getting late when Mummy Duck called her ducklings back to the safety of the pond.

But Sparrow kept on searching and searching and searching, until...

...finally she spotted some feathers sticking
up out of a clump of reeds.

It was Tufty!

"There you are!" Sparrow cried and rushed to give her friend a big feathery hug.

"What are you doing here?" asked Tufty.

"Looking for you! Everyone has been so worried about you." said Sparrow.

"Everyone?" asked Tufty in surprise.

"Yes, everyone! So can we please go home now," replied Sparrow.

The two friends set off together and were almost home when...

"HELP!"

A hungry fox was after
Tufty's brothers and sisters.

"LEAVE THEM ALONE
YOU BIG BULLY!"
Tufty shouted.

The fox turned around and grinned a nasty grin.
"Oh, look," he laughed. "An ugly duckling
with a stupid hairdo!"

SPLASH!

"MY HAIRDO IS NOT STUPID!" cried Tufty. Then he
rushed straight at the fox, who was so surprised that he jumped
backwards and fell into the pond with a great big SPLASH!

The ducklings were amazed.

"That was very brave," they said.
"Thank you for saving us."

Then they all said the words that
the ugly duckling had been waiting
to hear for a very long time...

"We're sorry we were so mean to you before just because you don't look quite the same as us. You are our brave little brother and you're not an ugly duckling at all."

"Aren't I?" said Tufty

"No, you are not!" said his brothers and sisters.

"You are a... a...
...delightfully different duckling!"

Then with a happy "Quark!", Tufty (the delightfully different duckling) waddled all the way back home where he lived happily and differently ever after.

QUARK!

Next Steps

Show the children the cover again. When they first saw it, did they think that they already knew the story? How is this story different from the traditional story?

Tufty the duck was different from his brothers and sisters. In what ways was he different? Did Mummy Duck mind that he was different?

The other farm animals were not very kind to Tufty. Why were they mean? What did Mummy Duck call them? Do the children think it's ok to be mean to someone because they are different?

Ask the children how they think Tufty felt. How would they feel if everyone was being mean to them? Discuss what they should do if they think they are being bullied or someone else might be.

Who was the bravest: the big scary fox or the little duckling with the 'stupid hairdo'? What did the other ducklings learn about Tufty after he chased the fox away?

Tufty had a friend throughout the story called Sparrow. How was Sparrow a good friend? Talk to the children about the importance of friendship and sharing your feelings.

In the end, Tufty was known as a 'delightfully different duckling'. He was finally accepted by his brothers and sisters. Talk about why it is important that we meet different people, and how you should never change who you are because of the actions of someone else.